Sweet Dreams of the Wild

Poems for Bedtime

by Rebecca Kai Dotlich
illustrated by Katharine Dodge

WORDSONG

BOYDS MILLS PRESS

Text copyright © 1996 by Rebecca Kai Dotlich
Illustrations copyright © 1996 by Katharine Dodge

Published by Wordsong
Boyds Mills Press, Inc.
A Highlights Company
815 Church Street
Honesdale, Pennsylvania 18431
Printed in Mexico

Publisher Cataloging-in-Publication Data
Dotlich, Rebecca Kai.
    Sweet dreams of the wild / poems by Rebecca Kai Dotlich ; illustrations by Katharine Dodge.—1st ed.
[32]p. : col. ill. ; cm.
Summary : Poems for children about animals and where they sleep.
ISBN 1-56397-180-1
1. Children's Poetry, American. 2. Animals—Juvenile poetry. [1. Poetry, American. 2. Animals—Poetry.]
I. Dodge, Katharine, ill. II. Title.
811.54—dc20   1996   AC
Library of Congress Catalog Card Number 94-60259

First edition, 1996
Book designed by Tim Gillner
The text of this book is set in 14-point Palatino
The illustrations are done in color pencil
Distributed by St. Martin's Press

10 9 8 7 6 5 4 3 2 1

For Chad, because I believed in him.
For Lara, because she believed in me.
And for Steve, who believed it all.

—R.K.D.

To my parents with love,

—K.D.

As the moon unwinds its silver thread
And sleepy children climb in bed,
Sweet dreams are stirring in the air
As wild ones sleep—
Do you know where?

Hummingbird,
hummingbird,
where do you sleep?

I rest near the ivy
that hugs the wall,
in a teacup-sized nest
because I'm so small.
High in a tree
I weave a warm bed,
with cattail fluff
and cobweb threads.
I cuddle up tight
with sweet dreams of the wild,
and THAT'S where I sleep,
sleepy child!

Gray mouse,
gray mouse,
where do you sleep?

I sleep in the attic
of a house old and warm,
bunching up to a quilt
that's been tossed
and torn.
Scampering quick to capture
a place of my own,
I rest best when the cat
of the house isn't home.
I cuddle up tight
with sweet dreams of the wild,
and THAT'S where I sleep,
sleepy child!

Silver cat,
silver cat,
where do you sleep?

I curl half-moon on
the window seat,
plumped fat and round
is how I sleep.
I slump in a chair
where someone just sat,
for long, lazy naps
just because I'm a cat.
I cuddle up tight
with sweet dreams of the wild,
and THAT'S where I sleep,
sleepy child!

Red robin,
red robin,
where do you sleep?

I rest in a nest
built of twigs and string
with my head tucked under
a folded wing.
Under gables and eaves,
in the fork of a tree,
or a warm, empty mailbox
is home to me.
I cuddle up tight
with sweet dreams of the wild,
and THAT'S where I sleep,
sleepy child!

Black spider,
black spider,
where do you sleep?

I sleep in a web
of knitted threads,
woven of silk
in a flower bed.
On a thin, gauzy sheet
I sway in the air,
from a lilac bush
to the garden chair.
I cuddle up tight
with sweet dreams of the wild,
and THAT'S where I sleep,
sleepy child!

Caterpillar,
caterpillar,
where do you sleep?

I wrap in a robe
of silky threads,
the quiet cocoon
is my growing bed—
Curled under the moon
and cradled in green,
wishing for shimmering
butterfly wings.
I cuddle up tight
with sweet dreams of the wild,
and THAT'S where I sleep,
sleepy child!

Red ladybug,
red ladybug,
where do you sleep?

I cling to the clover
soft and new,
or the petal of a rose
sprinkled light with dew.
Deep in the grass
of a green backyard—
a leaf for my bed,
and a blanket of stars.
I cuddle up tight
with sweet dreams of the wild,
and THAT'S where I sleep,
sleepy child!

Gray squirrel,
gray squirrel,
where do you sleep?

I curl in the hole
of a hollow tree,
or a ball-shaped nest
built strong with leaves.
Packed with twigs
and bits of bark,
my home is a cozy
den in the dark.
I cuddle up tight
with sweet dreams of the wild,
and THAT'S where I sleep,
sleepy child!

Black bat,
black bat,
where do you sleep?

I roost under bridges
and eaves of stone,
swaying upside down
by the crook of my toes—
Tucked in belfry towers high,
or deep in caverns
where I hide.
I cuddle up tight
with sweet dreams of the wild,
and THAT'S where I sleep,
sleepy child!

Green turtle,
green turtle,
where do you sleep?

I tuck deep inside
of my very own shell,
basking safe in the sand
is where I dwell.
I rest on a rock
or a moss-covered log,
near the edge of a puddle
at night in the fog.
I cuddle up tight
with sweet dreams of the wild,
and THAT'S where I sleep,
sleepy child!

White sheep,
white sheep,
where do you sleep?

I sleep in a flock
huddled close on a hill,
under starry skies
so dark and still.
In sweet, yellow straw
with a lamb at my side,
I nap in the open
countryside.
I cuddle up tight
with sweet dreams of the wild,
and THAT'S where I sleep,
sleepy child!

Brown bear,
brown bear,
where do you sleep?

I slumber in a cave
on a soft dirt floor
with the cold wind knocking
at my door.
Bundling furry-deep down
for a long winter's nap,
I nestle with blankets of brown
on my back.
I cuddle up tight
with sweet dreams of the wild,
and THAT'S where I sleep,
sleepy child!

Mountain goat,
mountain goat,
where do you sleep?

I nestle on mountaintops
cold and bare,
wrapped in a shawl
of warm, woolly hair—
High in a hollow
where bluebells grow,
in a winter wonderland
of snow.
I cuddle up tight
with sweet dreams of the wild,
and THAT'S where I sleep,
sleepy child!

Sea otter,
sea otter,
where do you sleep?

I nap off the shores
of the rocky sea,
sailing smooth on my back
in blue waters deep.
Near the coast
where a lighthouse
beckons stray boats,
in masses of seaweed and kelp
I float.
I cuddle up tight
with sweet dreams of the wild,
and THAT'S where I sleep,
sleepy child!

Sleepy child,
sleepy child,
where do you sleep?

Do you sleep in a bed
fluffed cozy and warm
with a white woolen quilt
and a bear in your arms?
Cold toes bundled and tucked
into night,
to the tender, warm hush
of a lullaby—
Do YOU cuddle up tight
with sweet dreams of the wild,
is THAT where you sleep,
sleepy child?

...Now sleepy children are snug in bed,
And the moon still shines its silver thread.
Sweet dreams are stirring in the air
As wild ones sleep—
And you know where.
Goodnight, sleepy child,
Goodnight.